A GHOST OF A CHANCE

BRIMSTONE INC.

ABIGAIL OWEN

DEDICATION

To: J.C., L.A., Sharon, & Maureen

A GHOST OF A CHANCE

He might just be the death of her...

Josie has a problem. Her brother's ghost shows up at her home and tells her if she doesn't save his life, he'll remain a ghost forever. But she can't save him on her own, not when his body was somewhere in the mountain wilderness near their home. Unfortunately, the man she walked away from— who she'd once wrapped hopes of her future around–is the only person who can help. The problem? He can't see ghosts and has no idea she can. So how does she convince him to help without giving away her secret?

CHAPTER 1

JOSIE BARTON RAISED HER HAND, shook it to try to stop the trembles, then knocked briskly at the door.

She winced. These new iron doors were gorgeous, but they sure hurt like hell to bang on. Not that that was where her focus should be. She knew she was mentally stalling for what came next.

After a long moment of silence, she glanced at her brother, who stood beside her. Hovered, more like. "He's not here," she hissed out of the side of her mouth.

The overcast skies were a constant grey, providing a vague drizzle which had her hair curling damply on her neck. Despite the waterproof windbreaker she wore over her t-shirt and jeans, her clothes clung uncomfortably to her skin. The only thing making this soggy day tolerable was the fresh smell of the wet pine woods prevalent in their area of Montana. She'd always loved that scent.

"He's working in the back bedroom. Try again." Peter didn't bother to lower his voice. He didn't need to. No one else would be able to hear him.

Reluctantly, she knocked again, having already confirmed that the doorbell didn't work.

A small, selfish part of her hoped Bryce wasn't home. Comfortable was not a word she associated with being around this man. Not because of her massive crush when they were teenagers. This new tension between them was more recent. Although, every so often, she'd catch a strangely intent look directed her way—as though he still cared if she didn't know better.

But she did know better. She'd made it that way.

With a deep breath, Josie pushed those thoughts away. Her brother needed her help, and she couldn't help him without Bryce.

Peter's pale form floated through her, and a cold shiver ripped up Josie's spine, causing instant brain freeze. "Quit that," she mumbled with a glare.

He flashed a wicked grin, still an ass even when spectral. "When Bryce comes to the door, tell him about me—"

"I'm not telling him *that*." She practically snarled the words. "And how are you so cheerful right now?"

He shrugged. "Maybe turning into a ghost disconnects your emotions?" He was guessing. Besides, she'd met plenty of ghosts who tapped into deep wells of emotion—love, regret, anger. Especially the anger. A better bet was Peter was trying to shield her from the worst of his predicament, downplaying the urgency even when his life hung on the line. Protecting her was a habit left over from childhood. The more serious the situation, the goofier he tended to get.

"I'm just saying, he'll understand," Peter insisted.

Josie highly doubted it. Most people wouldn't understand, but telling Bryce Evans she could see and speak to ghosts would lead to questions from her past she didn't want to answer. Mister Know-it-all Outdoorsman Local Hero didn't know everything. She wanted to keep it that way. Had to. To protect him from himself.

"Tell him," Peter urged.

She snapped her head around so hard her ponytail smacked her in the face, curls the color of wet sand damp and stinging. She aimed a glare at her brother that should've melted him into plasma goo on the spot. "Shut up."

"Excuse me?"

Josie froze at the sound of the deeply voiced question from the man now standing in the open doorway, then grimaced.

Peter smirked. "Now you *have* to tell him, or he'll think you're crazy."

Bryce already did.

Slowly Josie turned to face the man who managed to make desire coil around her heart even as trepidation coiled in her belly. With effort, she tried to arrange her face in a smile. It had been a while since she'd used the expression and it went down like castor oil.

Bryce frowned.

You need his help.

With a quick once-over she took in the fact that he wore a white t-shirt paired with jeans, a tool belt slung low around his hips. His dark hair was spiked as though he'd been running his hands through it repeatedly. *Damn.* Did drool run down her chin? How could a sweaty carpenter be so darn appealing?

"Why do I need to shut up?" he asked.

"Not you," she murmured, trying not to look away with the guilt of a school kid caught out in a lie.

His thick brows, already lowered, smoothed and his expression turned to the cool, emotionless mask he habitually wore in her vicinity. The same expression she gave him most of the time. "Is there something you need, Josie?"

"Only your undying devotion," Peter intoned in a high voice, batting his eyelashes.

Had he been living instead of a ghost, she would've punched him. Instead, she ignored him. You'd think her brother was twelve instead of twenty-five.

"Peter's in trouble. I need your help." She resisted the urge to clap her hand over her mouth. She hadn't meant to blurt that out, but Peter's juvenile antics and being near Bryce had rattled her. They'd tended to avoid each other since she'd moved back to her hometown.

Bryce eyed Josie closely, as though deciding how seriously to take her request. "Where is he?"

Only years of ignoring ghosts kept her from glancing in her brother's direction now. "Peter decided to do the Big Creek to Bear Creek Traverse. Alone."

Bryce crossed his arms, planting his feet wide, expression grim. "Not too smart."

"Hey," Peter protested.

Bryce, unable to hear or see him, continued. "But we've done that trek many times. I'm sure he's fine. If that's all, I'm a little busy—"

He went to close the door.

Josie choked as her lungs seized, panic kicking her adrenaline into high gear. She shot out a hand to stop him from shutting her out.

She wasn't getting through to Bryce. She'd known he wouldn't want to listen to her. The shaking in her hands increased—fear for her brother threatening to drag her under—and she fisted her hands to stop it. What could she say to get his help?

"Please." Desperate, she reached out and grabbed his arm without thinking, the first time she'd voluntarily touched the man in six years.

After what had happened a little over a year ago with that

ghost—the one with the blue eyes, the one who'd attacked her—she'd shut Bryce out. For his sake. After that, she'd shut everyone in her life out, too. Except her family, who knew her gift, understood. But pushing Bryce away with lies...that had been harder.

Now, the warmth of his skin under her fingertips, the rasp of his hair on her palm, penetrated the urgency driving her and produced a calming effect. Like reality and a solid human form had grounded her. Which was damn idiotic. "Something is wrong. I know it."

Bryce stiffened at her touch and glanced down at her hand.

Josie slowly drew back.

"I'm sure he's fine," he repeated. "When did he leave?"

"Yesterday."

"The Traverse takes three days, so he'll be back in two more."

Josie bit her lip against the sting of threatening tears. The coppery taste of her own blood slid across her tongue. Crying never helped anyone. "You don't understand. He's in trouble."

The vehemence in her voice wasn't like her, and something in his eyes softened. He reached out, and she thought for a second he might cup her face. But his gaze cooled because they didn't have that kind of relationship anymore, and he dropped his hand to his side. "Did he take a satellite phone with him?" he asked.

"Not this trip," Peter murmured in her ear. "Forgot it."

Josie gritted her teeth, tempted to lie, but she was never that convincing. "No."

"Then how do you know?" Bryce asked.

This conversation headed nowhere. "I just know. Will you help me?"

Josie's frustration grew as he stood there thinking. Not

his fault that Bryce pushed many of her buttons in ways she didn't seem to be able to shut down, and she struggled to bottle up her reaction like a shaken soda can.

Meanwhile, Bryce watched her like a scientist studying a specimen. Completely dispassionate, expression a mask, eyes a blank. "Let's slow down here."

"In other words, no. You won't help me." After her behavior, she didn't expect him to, but it still hurt.

She narrowed her eyes at the ghostly figure of her brother. He now stood behind Bryce, waving at her frantically over his shoulder. Subtly shifting her gaze, Josie did her best not to let the flesh and blood man see her reaction—disappointment laced with pure gut-wrenching terror. How was she going to do this on her own? "Thanks anyway," she muttered.

Josie walked away, her mind already spinning with her next steps. Peter could help her...tell her what to do and where to go.

"Why do you suddenly care?" Bryce called.

She froze at the question. Was that what Bryce really thought? That she didn't care about her family? She didn't turn, addressing her answer over her shoulder. "I've always cared."

Bryce's new house was still under construction. What would eventually be the driveway was currently a quagmire of mud from all the rain western Montana had received lately. Josie slogged across the unpaved yard and hopped into her four-wheel-drive. She jammed the key in the ignition when a knock sounded at her driver-side window. She jumped, glanced over and discovered Bryce outside.

She impatiently stabbed the button to lower the window. "What?"

"You're going to wait for Peter to come back, right?"

Once upon a time, real caring would have driven that

question. Not anymore, she was sure. This time she managed to smile sweetly and lie through her teeth. "Of course."

Without another word, she cranked the engine and drove away.

"You lied to Bryce."

Josie flinched at Peter's accusatory tone, though she didn't take her eyes from the road.

"Someone has to save your butt." She tightened her hands on the wheel and pressed harder on the gas.

"But you can't save me on your own."

An unhelpful observation if ever there was one. "If I'd said I planned to go after you alone, he would've tried to stop me. You don't have time for me to deal with the hassle."

Peter had no argument. Even he knew Bryce had a hero complex a mile wide. "What's the plan?"

"I assume you have extra camping gear at your house?"

"Yes."

She tapped her fingers on the steering wheel. "Then lead me to you. Only I'll be smart enough to remember the satellite phone to call for help."

Josie hoped like hell none of the thousand things that could go wrong with this plan did.

CHAPTER 2

BRYCE WATCHED as Josie drove calmly away. Watching her car disappear around the bend bugged him in a weird way. Since she'd broken things off over a year ago—before things had really got started—the rare times they ran into each other she showed no emotions. But this had been different, and he couldn't put his finger on how. A frown of concern tugged at his brow while irritation poked at him. She'd been adamant Peter was in danger but had no proof. Bryce knew his best friend well. They had done countless backpacking trips. Peter was probably just fine.

Josie's unusual behavior concerned him more. Despite living in her hometown, where her family had been for generations, they were lucky if she put in an appearance at major holidays.

Okay, she didn't live in town, exactly. She worked from home about ten miles out on a couple of solitary acres. Something to do with computers, which was no surprise, though her family didn't seem quite sure of the specifics. They all worried about her, out there alone. But Josie didn't seem to give a flying fig. If anything, when she deigned to appear in public, her "fuck off" vibes got louder.

The Bartons had practically adopted him after his parents passed away, and he'd never met a kinder group of people.

How anyone could be so standoffish with people who loved them stupefied Bryce. Especially Josie, who'd been so close and loving with her family before. The sweet girl he'd fallen for as a teenager disappeared only to be replaced by a distant, sullen woman. After the shove off, he'd tried a couple times to get her to talk to him, concerned, and been shut down harder each time.

The only thing that had kept him from pushing harder was the fact that her family didn't act concerned. After a while, he'd stopped asking them about her as well. He should have given up on her by now, but every time he saw her, he hoped...

Damn.

He shoved that last thought away. He didn't hope anything. Not anymore.

Bryce shook his head at the cloud of mist still lingering like a ghost in the wake of her utility vehicle and stalked inside. Hammer in hand, he returned to work on framing the back bedroom closet. A frustrated sound escaped his throat, and he stopped, mid-pound.

A nagging unease pulled at the center of his chest and refused to subside. Maybe Josie's concern for her brother had communicated itself to Bryce? Or perhaps the sensation resulted from a gut-level instinct insisting that she intended to ignore his implied advice to wait and, instead, head out on her own? Either way, he couldn't ignore the feeling.

"Damn."

With another shake of his head, he put down his tools and pulled out his cell phone but was automatically sent to Josie's voicemail.

Right.

Purpose drove his steps, along with a sense of urgency. He needed to pack his supplies and, hopefully, beat Josie to the trailhead. An uncomfortable premonition told him she planned to go there, despite her assurance that she wouldn't.

Without realizing he did so, Bryce started making plans. He and Josie would camp at the trailhead tonight, but then he'd head out—alone—in the morning.

Mid-way to the garage, where he kept his gear, Bryce changed direction. First, he had a phone call to make.

NIGHT FELL by the time Bryce reached the trailhead, but at least the drizzly morning had turned sunny by mid-day, resulting in a myriad of stars twinkling overhead once the sun disappeared. The ground, still damp from the earlier rain, squelched beneath his hiking boots as he walked, but it would be dry and firm by tomorrow. He found Peter's truck and set up camp in a clearing not far away.

Luck was with him—Josie had yet to arrive. Or perhaps he was wrong, and she'd listened to him. Just in case, though, Jared Nicholls, another camping buddy, had agreed to head up to the end of the trail on the likelihood Peter showed up there in the next day or so, or Josie decided to start there and work her way backward. Last check, no Josie and no Peter at either spot.

The flash of headlights illuminating the trees signaled the arrival of another person. Most serious backpackers, and they had to be serious to tackle this trail, arrived before dark to set up camp while they still had decent light. This had to be Josie. Sure enough, her red SUV entered the small dirt clearing that served as a parking area. Bryce waited, arms crossed, as she parked, turned off the engine, then sat inside a long moment.

Was she deciding how to deal with him? Probably.

Due to the tinted glass of her SUV, combined with the dark of night, he couldn't see what she was doing. The vehicle door slammed, alerting him that she'd gotten out. She stepped around the back as she came to where he stood, stopped a few feet away and crossed her arms. "What are you doing here?"

Why did her question make him feel like a party crasher caught in the act? Her wariness bothered him. "I decided to help after all."

"I see." She popped open the back of her utility vehicle, swinging the spare tire out of the way before yanking the door wide to unload. Well-packed camping gear appropriate for this kind of backpacking, he noted with surprised approval. Everything she would need for a trip like this.

"I didn't know you backpacked."

Josie shot him a glance. "I don't."

"Then where'd you get this stuff?"

"Peter's."

"If you don't backpack, how'd you know what to grab?"

Another quick glance, as though she was assessing him or something. "Lucky, I guess."

He resisted the urge to run a hand through his hair and snarl his frustration at her, trying to give her leeway because that worried little ridge was still between her brows. But why did she always have to be so cagey with him? Was she worried he'd make another pass? He'd got the message. She wasn't interested.

As she reached for a familiar canvas pouch, Bryce stepped closer and put a hand over hers. She jerked away from his touch, which only irritated him more, and she opened her mouth. Before she could say anything, he beat her to it. "You won't need the tent."

She raised a single eyebrow. "Oh?"

"I have a two-man tent already set up."

He caught her cryptic look, the way she glanced over his shoulder, and again got the distinct impression she waged some sort of internal debate.

"Okay."

His lips twitched at her grudging acceptance. Though how he could be amused baffled him. After all, he had come to help, and she acted as though his presence annoyed her. Once upon a time Josie would've smiled sweetly, thanked him, and acted happy to see him. He used to live for that smile. The memory so clear in his mind, the morose woman in front of him was almost painful to see instead.

Not for the first time, he wondered why her family wasn't worried about this change in her personality? Or maybe she was easier with them when he wasn't around. Why did he still care? He should be over this. Over her. She clearly was. Shrugging off his disappointment, Bryce hefted her pack. "Come on."

Josie grabbed her sleeping bag and followed. In silence, they set her up in the tent. After she assured him she had eaten dinner on the way up, Bryce rigged her food, hanging it from a tree with his, away from where they slept. In no time at all, they both lay in their sleeping bags in the darkened tent.

While the clouds had cleared, the moon remained hidden this time of the month. Far away from the ambient light cast by towns and cities, the darkness closed in on them.

"I'd like to leave as early as possible." Her soft voice floated across the space between them, wrapping around him, mingling with the sounds of the night.

The husky timbre still held uncanny sway over his body.

Bryce shifted to relieve his discomfort and tried to focus on her comment. "I have my watch alarm set to go off at 5:30 a.m."

"Good."

Based on the shuffling sounds, she'd flipped over and turned her back to him.

"Why are you so sure?" Bryce asked. The question had been bothering him since she'd shown up at his door.

Another rustle told him she faced his way. "About?"

Stalling. Definitely stalling.

"Pete's needing help. How do you know?" Her insistence that something was wrong, with seemingly zero evidence, had bugged him ever since she'd shown up at his house. Just like when they were teenagers. Josie always managed to know things she shouldn't. She only ever offered a mysterious smile at his questions. It drove him nuts.

A thump told him she had flopped back down. "You wouldn't believe me if I told you," she grumbled.

"Try me."

Silence greeted his dare, and Bryce held his breath.

For whatever strange reason, he wanted her to confide in him, trust him as she once did. He used to be the first person she brought her problems to. There'd always been something about Josie that got to him, triggered his protective side. Hell, practically brought out the need to don a cape.

Which only made the change in her harder to bear, because it went against who she'd been before that, the heart she'd once shown him.

"Goodnight, Bryce."

He blew out the breath he'd held, disappointment pressing him down into his sleeping bag. "Night."

A long beat of silence, then… "Bryce?"

"Yeah?"

A long sigh reached him in the dark. "Thanks," she murmured.

Bryce's chest tightened at the smallness of her voice. Suddenly, he was glad he'd come, and not just to stop her from doing something stupidly dangerous.

CHAPTER 3

Josie was in trouble.

Noticing Bryce's toned backside as he hiked ahead of her had to be completely inappropriate at this moment in time. Her brother was a damn ghost, dying somewhere out here. The combination of attraction and worry had her feeling twitchy, but how could she look away with said butt directly in her face?

Granted, she'd always been hyper-aware regarding the perfection that was Bryce's body—broad shoulders, trim waist, and six-pack that begged to be stroked. Every woman in town, even the taken ones, unanimously acknowledged that his dark hair, warm brown eyes, strong jaw, and deep voice made Bryce a welcome star in many a sexual fantasy. Didn't help that he was also smart, genuinely nice—even when he was stone-faced the few times they'd encountered each other—and occasionally funny. He'd been starring in her fantasies for a long time, despite this past year and telling her heart and mind and body he was now strictly hands off.

Josie gave herself a mental slap. *Quit it. He thinks you're a first-rate jerk, and you aren't allowed to like him. Anymore.*

Not after that blue-eyed ghost. That attack had put the fear of God into her that she would bring a similarly malevolent spirit down on someone she truly cared about.

"If you put the kind of focus you're using on my best friend's ass, you would definitely have found me by now!" a laughing masculine voice interrupted her thoughts.

Careful since Bryce was still turned away, she flicked a glance at the spectral image of her brother.

Peter hovered alongside her and rolled his eyes. "Of course not. What was I thinking? You don't love him anymore."

Her brother saw too much. As a girl, Bryce had been her own personal hero. She'd gone off to college and thought she'd outgrown those girlish feelings. Then, last summer before she'd moved away, they'd spent a day together fishing. He'd kissed her. Not a chaste kiss either, but one that surpassed every girlish fantasy she'd pinned on him. She'd hoped….

No. That fish had gotten away and swum far down the river. So why did she still blush when she caught one of those intense stares of his? Because she was into self-torture apparently.

Peter flipped around to float backwards and peered into her face. "Unless you secretly still have a crush."

Josie snorted and hoped he believed it.

Bryce paused and glanced over his shoulder at her. "Problem?"

She swatted a hand around. "Bug."

Peter laughed, the sound pinging around her in the oddest way, as though it had no single source. "I resemble that remark," he said.

Unaware of the byplay between her and Peter, Bryce nodded. "Let's stop for a water break here."

"Okay."

Josie unclipped the hip and chest straps, swung Peter's large pack off her back and rolled her shoulders, grateful to be free of the weight. If she wasn't focused on saving her brother or on her distracting traveling companion, Josie would've paused to appreciate her surroundings. On the eastern side of the Bitterroot mountains, the trail lay before them in the form of a sun-dappled forest floor. Pine trees surrounded them with green, giving off a fresh scent, the wind sounding like rain as it rustled the needles.

With a tug she pulled her water bottle out of the side pouch on her pack and took a long, parched swig. Glancing over the end of her bottle, she found Bryce watching her. Her stomach dipped, and, immediately, heat shot through her veins, travelling through her blood, intent on pooling low. But damned if she'd let him see how he affected her. Raised eyebrows asked her question.

Bryce's expression subtly shifted back to neutral and he gestured to her pack. "You've managed to hang with me pretty well."

Damn good thing, because Bryce had tried to leave her at camp this morning. The problem was he needed her. He just didn't know it yet.

Peter's body lay somewhere off the path, and his ghost had to lead her to him.

"I guess jogging really does help." In truth she ran five to ten miles every day. With no friends, no close neighbors, and no social life, what else did she have to do?

He brushed a streak of dirt off his shorts. "Why don't you like me?"

Josie choked as water went down the wrong pipe and then choked more when Bryce thumped on her back like a bass drum. He hadn't touched her in years, and this is what she got?

Eventually she caught her breath, holding up a hand to

indicate she was okay. She eyed the man in front of her. Did she dare tell him the truth about her abilities? About why she knew where Peter was? About how she'd loved him forever and wished things could be different? That might not be a fabulous idea with them stuck in the wilderness together. On the other hand, he couldn't run away either. She'd have to clue him in eventually.

"I like you fine Bryce. I always have. I admire you even."

His expression shut down. "Because I saved that girl?"

Six months ago a young girl had gotten lost in the mountains, and Bryce found her. His knowledge of the area, combined with quick thinking, ultimately saved her life. But, like now, he was touchy about it. The man never could take recognition or compliments well.

Amusement tickled inside her chest. He never could take a compliment. Josie crossed her arms and leaned back against an outcropping of rock. "Because you've been a good friend to Peter and lovely to my family. You're also a man of your word, and you don't shy away from hard work or the truth."

Not to mention you hit every yes button my body has.

Bryce blinked several times, as if not entirely sure how to take her honesty. "Then why the cold shoulder all the time?"

Was he seriously bringing this up now? What could she say that would make it easy to continue to keep her distance in the future? "I guess... I figured after…"

She paused trying to word it right.

"After you categorically told me that nothing romantic would happen between us ever?" he asked, almost casually.

She cleared her throat. "I figured you didn't like me anymore. As friends, I mean."

"I like you fine, Josie." He tossed the words back at her. "I just don't like how you treat your family these days."

Yeah. I don't either. Josie sighed, put away her water, and hitched the pack up over her shoulders. "I love my family, Bryce."

"You sure don't act like it."

That smarted. She didn't bother to hide her wince. "You've asked me that before," she said.

After breaking things off, she'd moved back to her hometown, to her current setup in the middle of the woods. He'd visited her on several occasions. Checking up on her, worried about her, he'd said.

"And you told me to butt out."

"That hasn't changed," she muttered, glancing away, hating to do this all over again. It hurt every time.

"Why?"

Josie shook her head, lips flat. "Let me ask you this... Has my family ever acted like I was in the wrong?"

He cocked his head as though seriously considering the question. "They're disappointed any time you don't show up."

"But are they angry? Blaming?"

"No." He drew the word out.

"Then maybe you should let it go." She wasn't angry with him. How could she be angry with caring. Josie was just...sad. Exhausted, mentally, physically, and any other -ly.

Bryce finished clipping his belly and chest straps. "Your family was good to me after..." He looked down, then back up at her. "I don't like to see them hurt."

Staying away hurts me as much as them. Maybe more, because I'm alone. They have each other.

"Or you. You seem..." He glanced away.

Pathetic? Selfish? "What?"

Bryce pinned her with that intense look that stole her breath. "Lonely."

Oh. He had her nailed. His open concern—for her alone— could get dangerously attractive. Instead of answering, she waved at the trail. Thankfully, he took the hint and they continued in thick silence.

Two hours later, Josie felt like a wrung out mop. Her legs screamed from the constant upward climb, her lungs protested the lack of oxygen, and sweat poured off her body, salty in her mouth and stinging her eyes.

"Stop!" Peter yelled.

She squeaked in surprise at Peter's sudden appearance.

"You okay?" Bryce called from ahead.

"Fine," she called back. "Why are we stopping?" she hissed at Peter.

"This is where I went off trail. Time to tell Bryce."

Crap. She'd spent the long hours of walking stressing over an explanation for how she knew where to find Peter. The metaphorical light bulb that should be going off in her head apparently had faulty wiring because no plausible ideas had struck.

She knelt and pretended to tie her hiking boot. "He won't believe me," she muttered low.

"Who won't believe you?" Bryce had doubled back and towered over her on the trail.

Josie glanced at Peter, who unhelpfully shrugged. She sighed. "Peter's not that way."

"The trail goes this way." He took a step in the direction he indicated.

She hopped up and moved into his path, both hands out to stop him. Yup. That six pack was for real and not just in her head.

She pointed in the other direction. "He went off trail."

Bryce sent her a skeptical frown and scouted the ground, at a guess for any sign of Peter. "And you know this how? Did you become some kind of tracking expert recently?"

Josie shuffled her feet, kicking at a rock on the trail.

"Tell him," Peter urged.

"No," she said to both of them. "But he did go this way."

Peter groaned. "Just tell him."

"Shut up," she muttered out the side of her mouth.

Bryce's eyebrows flew high. "I didn't say anything."

"Not you." She knew that look. The *you should be locked up* look. Adrenaline surged. *Oh God. Am I really going to have to do this?*

Keeping her gift a secret from him was part of keeping him safe. But every "What if?" was outweighed by her brother's life. And it was too late. She had run out of ideas and options.

"You're not making any sense," Bryce said. The real concern in his eyes actually had her wanting to wrap her arms around him and just be. Let her worries go. Pretend she had a real friend in him. The one she'd been missing.

Josie rubbed her forehead. "I know."

Peter became so agitated he shimmered. "Tell him!"

"I will," she snapped at her brother. Then turned to face a watchful and rightfully concerned Bryce. Josie licked her lips. "I don't know any way to ease you into this..."

Bryce crossed his arms, the impressive muscles straining the material of his t-shirt. "Tell me."

Straight shooter. Bryce had always been that way. "I see ghosts."

She held still and waited for a reaction, any reaction. Her heart jumped into her throat, cutting off her air. He knew now. Bryce finally knew. After all these years. *Please let him believe me.*

After a long second, he blew out a breath. "Okay."

And there it was. Her heart dropped from her throat to the pit of her stomach with a thud. He thought her certifiable. Josie held up a hand. "It's a family gift. All of us have it to one extent or another, but I'm...particularly gifted."

"All of you see ghosts." He laughed. The damn man

laughed at her. Obviously, Bryce didn't believe her.

Panic fluttered inside her chest. She needed him to believe her or Peter would be dead. "Yes."

"And you see a ghost right now?"

She swallowed but nodded. "Peter's ghost."

Anger and a very real concern that possibly bordered on alarm replaced amusement and pulled Bryce's brow down. "I'm up here because Peter's ghost is talking to you?"

She lifted her chin, facing him down. "Yes. He's in trouble."

He scrubbed a hand over his face, eyes closed, and shook his head.

Holy shit, he doesn't believe me. He thinks this is some horrible prank or something.

Josie tripped as she tried to step closer. With fumbling fingers, she unclipped her pack and dropped it to the ground so she wouldn't be hampered, then wrapped her fingers around his wrists, tugging his hands away from his face. "I'm not making this up."

He said nothing, but opened his eyes, staring at her.

"Peter?" she called. "A little help?"

Peter hovered in front of Bryce. "Tell him I'm sorry about Jenny Patton."

"What does that mean?" she asked.

"Just tell him."

She huffed. "Peter says he's sorry about Jenny Patton."

Bryce stepped back so abruptly she jerked with him. "When did he tell you?" he demanded.

She scurried back to put some space between her and a rightfully upset man. "Just now. What happened with Jenny Patton?" Irrational jealously twanged.

"We both wanted to take her to Homecoming—" He cut off the explanation and unleashed a growl of irritation before marching away.

Crap. Crap. Crap. She had to pull out the big guns. "I saw your parents shortly after they died," she called after his retreating back.

Bryce spun around and stalked back toward her, unbuckling his pack as he moved. Josie tried to stand her ground, but didn't do a great job at it, scooting backward warily.

He didn't touch her but got right in her face. "Don't you dare bring my parents into this," he said, so quietly it hurt her heart more than if he had yelled.

Her heart fluttered around like a trapped bird in a cage. "It's true. They wanted me to tell you the crash wasn't your fault."

"Who said it was?"

"They knew you blamed yourself. You never told anyone, did you? But they knew."

White lines bracketed Bryce's mouth. "You're guessing."

Josie closed her eyes against the leashed pain in his expression. "Your mother also said not to worry about the vase you broke."

Silence. She opened her eyes to discover wary disbelief staring at her. Hope surged as she recognized a question in the dark eyes that searched her face.

She could do this. "I know it's hard to believe. But I'm telling the truth. More importantly, Peter needs our help. He can lead us to his body."

"Only about another hour away." Peter now floated around Bryce's shoulder.

"He says only another hour or so. Give me that long to prove it to you."

Bryce's chest heaved, and she had no doubt she was to blame for his turmoil. But she needed him.

"I'm still not sure I believe this. I'll give one hour." Bryce fiddled with his watch and it beeped.

Relief flooded through her. "Thank you," she whispered.

CHAPTER 4

BRYCE COULDN'T PEEL his eyes off Josie, even if he wanted to because she was ahead of him on the trail. Only he didn't want to. He'd always enjoyed looking at Josie. If anything, the familiar ache of attraction was his only anchor in a sea of unreality. He took the first fifteen minutes of their off-trail trek to simmer down from the anger, confusion, and disbelief buffeting him like a flash storm in the mountains.

This woman. His entire past, every moment, every odd hesitation or blink, was replaying in his mind. But especially the memory of the night she'd shut him out.

He'd arrived at her brand new house after weeks of not being able to keep that day fishing and the kiss they'd shared out of his mind. A surprise. A good one that he'd hoped might lead to…more between them. Something special.

She'd opened the door all wrapped up in a cozy sweater and turtleneck, and he would have sworn he saw a flash of joy in her eyes. But then it was gone. In the nicest, but strangely remote, way possible, she'd said that she'd thought of their kiss too, but that she wasn't interested in more. He was Peter's friend and that was all he'd ever be to her.

But then she'd moved back, and he'd thought they could at least be friends. That's when things had gotten weird, and then strained, between them.

Was it the ghosts that had changed her so much? Or maybe she was struggling with a mental disorder, and her family knew, and this was part of that.

Hell, he had no idea what to think.

"That way?" Josie half-whispered the question to an apparition he couldn't see. This was the fourth or fifth time she confirmed the direction.

She sent Bryce a nervous glance over her shoulder before moving off. Bryce followed in total silence. With each step, their hiking boots crunched on the bed of pine needles.

"Is Peter dead?" He didn't pull back the words. He didn't want to admit there could be truth to this situation, but at the same time, he had to know.

She glanced to his left and smiled. At Peter? "Not yet. According to him, he followed a ghost off trail."

He narrowed his eyes, skeptical. "Really?" He'd never seen Peter act erratically. Wouldn't he have noticed odd behavior in all of her family members if Josie told the truth?

"Peter isn't sure, but thinks he went over the side of a cliff." She checked with the blank spot above his left shoulder again. "He's unconscious. He says he can see his body. His left leg is badly broken."

Dread settled like a brick in his chest. Holy hell, now she was pulling him into the act, drawing him into her beliefs. This couldn't be real. She needed serious help, and he'd make sure she got it after he managed to get her back off this mountain.

He waved for her to keep walking. "Then we better move quickly."

After another minute or two of silent trekking, curiosity

got the better of him. "How long have you been able to talk to ghosts?"

"Since I was fourteen."

And he seventeen. His gut twisted as the implication of the timing hit him. "And you really saw my parents?"

She nodded, her ponytail bobbing up and down. "They were my first."

"Why didn't you say anything then?"

"Yeah, right. And tell you what? Your dead parents talked to me? You don't even believe me now."

A valid concern.

"I tried to convey their message in other ways," she said, more quietly.

Bryce startled. He didn't remember that. He reached out and stopped her with a hand on her arm, slick with sweat. "How?"

She searched his expression with something akin to hope in her steady, brown-eyed gaze. "Any chance I got, I tried to convince you none of it was your fault. Or on holidays, I'd mention how your parents were there with us, or watching over you. Birthday messages of pride and love."

Bryce rocked back, dropping his hand from her. The sudden lack of contact left him strangely empty. She *had* done that, often, a gesture he'd taken as pity at the time. His grief never allowed him to fully appreciate her attempts to ease his pain. Now the beauty of what she had tried to do struck him in the region of his heart, piling guilt and confusion onto the dread.

Bryce gave himself a mental shake. How was this real?

"We need to get going." Josie turned and plodded onward.

Bryce followed, no longer paying her butt as much attention, his mind working through snippets of half-remembered conversations. *Could she be telling the truth? No way.*

After a while of hiking silently, Josie slowed. "Peter says to be careful. He thinks we're close to where he fell."

They rounded a tree with thick underbrush blocking any view to the left and skidded to a halt at the edge of a steep drop-off. After they caught their breath, Josie dropped to her knees and peered over the edge. "Oh my God. I see him."

Bryce's heart slammed in his chest like a trapped bird beating against a cage. He leaned over her. Sure enough, Pete's bright red windbreaker flashed from a ledge about twenty-five feet below them.

"Shit." The word tumbled out of him. Then calm kicked in and he went into *git-it-done* mode.

He dropped his backpack on the ground behind him and yanked out the satellite phone he had brought just in case.

Jared, who still waited at the other end of the trail for Peter to show, answered immediately.

"911, buddy. We found Peter. He's hurt, badly broken left leg, unconscious, down on a ledge. Get in touch with the park rangers and round up fire and rescue. It's going to take a crew to get him down."

Jared was all business, asking a few questions for clarification. "I'll radio when I know more."

"Understood." After checking, Bryce relayed their coordinates.

"How long will all that take?" Josie asked after he radioed off, face deathly pale.

He brushed a finger against her cheek, suddenly needing the contact, and her eyes widened. "To get up here? It depends on how they do it. Likely by helicopter. Based on where we are, I'd say a few hours. Maybe more."

"Oh," she repeated in a broken whisper.

The urge to kiss her, tell her everything would be all right pulled at him, but the alarm on his watch went off with a loud beeping. The one he'd set when he'd given Josie an hour to find Peter's body. He stepped back as he hit the button to cancel it. Shaking off that urge, Bryce reached for his pack again to pull out more equipment. "I'm going to rappel down to check on Peter and see if I can't stabilize him."

"What can I do?"

"Set up the tent; it's not hard." He handed her his pack and gave her a gentle shove in the direction they'd come from. "We passed a small clearing back there." This rescue might take hours. No way were the two of them getting off this mountain tonight.

"Got it." She disappeared without a backward glance, all business.

Even while he set up his rope, anchoring it around the base of a large tree, Bryce still appreciated how she didn't panic or fuss. Like him, Josie was a doer. Take care of each task until the job was done.

In short order, Bryce prepared and rappelled down the rock face to where Peter had landed. His friend smelled of body odor and dirt. Closer now, he confirmed there was only a small amount of blood from a head wound. The leg, while grotesque, wasn't bleeding. A check of his pulse revealed it was steady, but faint. Nothing he could do about that though.

With the ledge not large enough to hold both of them, he had to work quickly. Bryce dangled from his own rope and assessed Peter's injuries.

As soon as he touched Pete's leg, a yelp from Josie echoed down to him, and then her head appeared over the ledge above him. "Peter said that hurt like a son of a bitch. What'd you do?"

"Barely touched his leg. Ghosts feel pain?"

Josie made a face. "He's the first non-dead ghost I've talked to, so I guess they can when still attached to a body."

Interesting. "Don't move the leg if I can help it. Got it. Tell Peter I have to secure him. It'll mean some jostling."

"He heard you." She disappeared again.

Fuck this is weird.

Working quickly, Bryce hammered a piton into a crack in the rock face as an anchor, then fed rope through, securing it around Peter as best he could, while trying not to move the injured leg. No mean feat when dangling several hundred feet above a nasty fall. He had confidence in his own gear, but what if Peter slipped while he was setting things up. Fear lodged like a boulder in his stomach, but his hands were rock steady.

One problem at a time.

When he had Peter as secure as he could make him, Bryce turned his attention to the next task—keeping his friend warm in the rapidly dropping temperatures as the shadows of evening approached. Based on previous experience, rescues could take hours, which meant they'd still be waiting in the cold of night, and Peter had already passed one relatively unprotected.

Peter's pack wasn't here. Not that he'd seen at least. Bryce twisted to search below, but a larger outcropping blocked most of his view.

"Josie!" Bryce watched above him for any sign she'd heard his call. After a long pause, he sucked in a lungful of air to get louder. "Jo—"

"Yeah?" She stuck her head over the edge.

Bryce expelled the rest of his breath like a burst balloon. "Peter's pack isn't here. Do you see it anywhere up there, or below?"

"I haven't seen it up here." Josie leaned further out over the ledge.

"Careful," he called, stomach and heart racing to see which could get out of his throat first.

She ignored him and shaded her eyes with her hand. "I see a flash of red. I think it's about a hundred feet below you."

Damn. She wouldn't like the alternative. "We have to keep him warm until the rescue crews arrive."

A pause greeted his words. "Is there a way for me to lower one of our sleeping bags down?"

That was easier than expected...or did she not realize that meant they'd be sharing a sleeping bag tonight? "There's another rope in my pack."

Fifteen minutes later, Peter was tucked in, warm and dry and as comfortable as he could be made without medical supplies. Bryce scaled up the mountain to where Josie waited.

"What next?" she asked as he stepped out of his climbing gear but left the rope in place in case they needed it later.

"Now we wait."

"I hate waiting," she muttered.

Me too.

CHAPTER 5

THE SUN HAD DIPPED below the horizon at least an hour ago, with no rescue team in sight. Josie shivered from the cold, despite being wrapped in a heavy jacket of Peter's she'd brought from his house. And a rock dug mercilessly into her ass, regardless of how many times she shifted positions, only adding to her discomfort.

A large hand, strong and capable, appeared in front of her, bearing a titanium mug-like container with a spoon sticking out of it at a wonky angle. She inhaled the aroma as he waved it under her nose. Smelled like beef stew. Her mouth watered.

"Here," Bryce said. "You need to eat."

Despite the fact that Peter's ghost stayed with her constantly, Josie had refused to leave his body. She sat on the ledge above where he lay.

"I'd tell you if something went wrong," Peter tried to tease.

She sent him a glare and pointed over the outcropping. "Don't joke about stuff like that when you're lying half-dead on a cliff."

He held up both see-through hands. "Fine. Fine. Stay with my body and be miserable."

Josie reached out and took the food from Bryce. A long day of hiking with a heavy pack sure helped a girl work up an appetite. Even through her thin gloves, the heat warmed her hands. "Thanks."

With a grunt, he dropped to the ground beside her and tried a couple ways to fold his legs before giving up and sticking them out straight. Like her, he had changed from shorts into cargo-style hiking pants and a thicker jacket. She watched his struggle to get comfortable, lips tipped in silent amusement.

"Any change?" Bryce asked.

She glanced over the edge. Good thing she wasn't afraid of heights. "No."

"And Peter's ghost is…?"

She shifted her gaze directly above his head.

Bryce angled his head to look into the trees above. "Dude, don't be a helicopter ghost."

Peter laughed as he floated away a foot or two. Josie smiled at Bryce's antics. She had missed that. The way he used to tease, make her laugh.

The phone rang, and Bryce's easy smile fell away. Josie fought the confusing combination of dismay at losing that brief shared moment of warmth and elation that the rescue must be moving forward.

After a quick conversation, Bryce hung up. "That was Jared. The helicopter should be here soon."

"Thank heaven," she breathed. The panic holding her chest in a vice since Peter had showed up at her house eased a tad.

"Yeah."

Bryce remained quiet while she ate, but for the first time in a long time, the silence between them wasn't awkward.

More…companionable. Josie chewed and tried not to let the sense of intimacy wrap seductive arms around her, tried not to remember the way Bryce's arms tenderly held her one hot summer night long ago.

The *thump, thump, thump* of a helicopter caught their attention. Bryce jumped to his feet and waved his flashlight to gain their attention. Within minutes, the craft had a spotlight on them. With no obvious landing area close by, two men with gear winched down to them. Then the pilot flew away.

"Wait," Josie said, not taking her gaze from it. "Where are they going?"

"To find a place relatively close by to land and wait until Peter can be stabilized and prepared for transport," Bryce explained.

Right.

Time went into fast forward from there, while at the same time slowing to a crawl. After describing the situation and what they'd done, she and Bryce watched the rescue team rappel down to Peter.

His ghostly form stood beside her. "What do you think my chances are?"

If there hadn't been a tightness to his voice, she would've taken the words as he meant, as a joke. Peter always tried to make things easier for her, but he was scared. So was she.

Together they watched as the rescue team worked carefully on the mountain face, but every time they moved him, the specter of her brother groaned. Josie wished she could take his hand, impart her support. But, if she tried to touch him, she'd just pass through and get a brain freeze headache.

Josie fidgeted with the zipper of her jacket, then jumped when Bryce reached over and took her hand, lacing their fingers together, his skin warm against hers despite the chill in the air. "He'll be okay."

She swallowed but didn't pull away. Couldn't. She needed his strength right now. "They're hurting him."

"They're saving his life."

Though miniscule, Bryce seemed to catch her nod.

"Do you think you'll remember any of this when you wake up?" she asked Peter.

Peter shrugged. "Your guess is as good as mine."

"Will he?" Bryce asked.

"We're not sure. As far as we know, no one in our family has seen anyone but the dead before." But she was the strongest of them with this gift.

"You said you're particularly gifted?"

Cursed more like. "It's different for each of us. Mom can see them but can't talk to them. Peter only catches glimpses now and then."

"Why don't you like it?"

Peter doubled over with a loud groan before she could answer. She didn't bother asking what had happened. She peeked over the ledge and saw they'd managed to maneuver his body from the ledge onto a sled-like device and strapped him down.

Peter slowly straightened. "Damn, that hurt. I hope I don't remember this when it's over."

Josie turned to respond and gasped. "Peter…"

"What?"

"You're fading," she whispered through pinched lips.

His image came through in patches now, like a Swiss cheese spirit. He held up his hands, peering at her through the holes. Holes that were growing in size. "Maybe I'm waking up because of the pain?"

"What's wrong?" Bryce asked beside her.

Josie realized she'd clamped down on his hand hard enough to cut off circulation. She loosened up, though she didn't release him. "His ghost is fading. He thinks maybe the pain is waking him up." She hoped that was true.

Bryce wrapped an arm around her. "I'm sure he's right."

"Josie?" Peter asked.

She stared at Peter's one visible eye as only fifty percent of him remained whole now.

She swallowed hard. "Yes?"

"Tell Mom and Dad—"

"Don't." Her whole body shook now. "Don't do that. Don't you dare say goodbye."

The corner of Peter's mouth quirked. "Okay. You know what I'd say anyway."

"You'll be fine."

And he was gone.

"Peter?"

Nothing.

"Peter?"

"Is he gone?" Bryce asked quietly.

She nodded, tears pushing at her eyes, burning. Tears she refused to let fall. With a tug, Bryce pulled her around and held her, which knocked her tenuous control right over the cliff with her brother, tears streaming down her cheeks. She tucked into him and just let the emotions run their course, buffeted by fear and hope and the terror of losing someone she loved.

"What if we were too late?" she mumbled into Bryce's chest.

"Don't think like that."

She pulled back and stared into her girlhood hero's handsome face, shadowed in dark, their only light his flashlight. The sound of the rising helicopter broke them apart

After a lot of maneuvering, Peter flew away with his rescuers. When the whirr of the blades faded in the distance, the only sound that remained was pine needles rustling in the wind.

Bryce tugged her away from the ledge. "We should try to get some sleep. Jared will pass on any news."

Josie allowed Bryce to lead her away from the cliff and back to their camp.

CHAPTER 6

JOSIE JUMPED as the ring of the satellite phone pierced the silence with a loud trill. After the helicopter left with Peter, with night well underway, they decided to stay where they were and head back down in the morning. Going through the motions, they cleaned up from dinner, hung their food, got ready for bed, and zipped themselves into Bryce's tent, where they sat on his sleeping bag, waiting for news.

Sleep was out of the question.

Heart in her throat, Josie listened to Bryce's side of the conversation. She didn't realize she was wringing her hands until he reached across the space between them to take one of hers in his own—large and warm and slightly callused. Why that small detail centered her, she didn't know.

"Thanks, Jared." He rang off.

"Well?" she asked, searching Bryce's expression for any clue.

"They're at the hospital now," he said gently. "Peter's in surgery for the leg."

She slumped forward. "Okay. Not dead." Thank God for that.

"You seem...disappointed?"

"I'm relieved." She looked up, searching for the words to describe her reaction. "I just can't...see him anymore. I don't know what that means."

Bryce gave the hand he still held a squeeze, calluses rough and comforting. "Pete's strong. He'll pull through."

She twisted a strand of her ponytail around one finger. "I'm sure you're right."

Josie blinked as Bryce chuckled. "What?"

"You still play with your hair when you're nervous."

"I guess I do." She unwound the strand and didn't know what to do with her hand because their linked ones were in her lap.

"Come on." Bryce released her and held open one side of the sleeping bag. Both of Peter's bags were now at the bottom of the mountain, which meant they had to share. "We still have to hike back down to the cars tomorrow. Let's get some sleep. I'll take the zipper side."

"Thanks." She wouldn't say no about the zipper side, since her body had already turned numb from the cold, and he was more used to this hiking stuff.

She slid inside. After turning off the electric lamp, he slipped in behind her, his body up against hers, her back to his broader front, because there wasn't room for anything different. She knew there was nothing sexual about it, but instantly she was wide awake and not cold anymore. Could he hear her heart thumping? Feel the way she was struggling to control her breathing.

Peter could be dying for, heaven's sake. She shouldn't be thinking these thoughts...

The rasp of the zipper sounded loud in the darkness and he scooted closer as it did. "I'm going to put my arm around you." His breath brushed against the back of her neck, sending shivers cascading down her spine.

Lord this was going to be a long night.

Josie cleared her throat. "You've gotta put it somewhere."

She lifted her arm, allowing him to drape his own across her stomach, and his subtle scent—like wood chips—wrapped around her. Would it be wrong to snuggle into him? Or, worse, rub up against him as if she were a cat and he catnip.

She needed a distraction. "Bryce?"

"Mm-hmmm?" His chest rumbled against her back.

Josie shivered—not in a cold way, in a delicious way. *Focus, woman.* "Thank you."

He was quiet a long moment. "You're welcome. Thank you for not giving up on Peter even when I didn't believe you."

She gave a small one-shoulder shrug...or tried to as his weight kind of pinned her down. "He's my brother."

He was quiet a moment. "I didn't come up here to help Peter, originally."

She twisted her neck but couldn't see his expression in the dark and gave up. "What do you mean?"

"I didn't believe he was in trouble. How could I?"

She snorted a laugh. "I wasn't exactly rational with the explanations."

The fact that they could talk at all this way was a change. A breakthrough. Only a breakthrough wasn't a good thing. When Peter was better and this was all over, she needed things to go back the way they were. Being around her...it still wasn't safe. For anyone.

"I came up to stop you from doing something stupid," he confessed, and she could hear the cringe in his voice.

See. Bryce was always trying to protect her. If he knew the truth, then he'd want to stay involved, and she couldn't risk that. Tonight, she needed to keep things casual.

"I'd be mad if you weren't so darn right," she murmured. An attempt at teasing.

He huffed a laugh. The tickle of it rolled across her nerve endings.

Nice laugh. She didn't hear it often, and never because of her. "You were amazing."

His turn to semi-shrug. "I only did what I could think of to help."

"I would've been useless on my own. At least I brought Peter's satellite phone, but no rope. I wouldn't have been able to get to him."

"He made it overnight on the ledge without any protection. Likely he would've been fine."

"Hopefully he doesn't develop pneumonia from the exposure." She shifted against the worry creeping back into her head. "And you need to learn how to take a compliment."

"Maybe." His arm tightened around her, and her sweatshirt shifted up, exposing a sliver of skin.

Could he tell his pinky finger pressed against bare flesh now? Josie held her breath, trying not to move, and he didn't move or react, so she did her best to not think about it. But not thinking about his touch was impossible. Not when every repressed desire where this man was concerned reared its ugly head and whispered at her to raise the shirt a little higher.

Distraction. "Do you remember when I ended up in the hospital when I was eighteen?"

Bryce tensed. "Yes. You were attacked on campus at college. He almost crushed your windpipe. I've never seen bruises that black." Traces of old concern laced his voice. God, she'd missed the way he used to care about her.

Then his words sank in and Josie sucked in a breath, and his fingers came into contact with more skin at her midriff.

"I didn't realize you came to see me in the hospital. Why don't I remember?"

"I don't know. I visited a couple times." He held something back. She could tell.

"Oh." She licked her lips, wondering how he'd take her next words. Sharing wasn't something she did often. "I wasn't attacked by a live person."

Glowing blue eyes had haunted her nightmares for several years after that. But she hadn't known just how bad things were until she'd gotten her first job and moved away from home. When Bryce had showed up to surprise her, she'd been thankful for the winter weather, because she'd been covered from head to toe. What he hadn't seen under those clothes were the healing bruises from a second attack.

His grip tightened. "A *ghost* did that to you?"

She squeezed her eyes shut at the rasp of combined anger and incredulity in his voice. Not with her, but for her. It had been so long since Bryce had been on her side. She'd missed depending on him to have her back, and the way that made her feel—protected, cherished, special. "Yes."

"But no one else in your family has been hurt like that, though, right?"

"No. I'm stronger in the gift, so I tend to attract more spirits. I enjoyed it at first, talking to the ghosts who visited me, or the ones I stumbled across if they were attached to a certain place. For the most part, they were nice. Helpful even. Your father got me through a history test my freshman year of college I would have failed otherwise."

He jerked, exposing even more of her skin. "Dad helped you cheat?"

She grinned at his heavy skepticism. "Yup. I like your father."

His chest rose and fell with a silent exhale. "Do you still see him? Or Mom?"

Slowly she shook her head. "Not for a while. I've stopped letting ghosts anywhere near me."

Silence. Was he thinking about that? Regretting what she'd shared? "To protect yourself?" he finally asked.

"Yes."

"Is that why you live alone?"

"Yes."

"And avoid your family?" His voice took on an edge of intensity. Maybe this was not the distraction she should have used.

But Bryce was smart. She should have been more honest with herself and acknowledged that he would have arrived at this conclusion eventually. Besides, she was tired of keeping it from him.

Or maybe she was just weak, because her resolve from minutes ago was already crumbling.

"Yes," she confessed. "They still see ghosts. Attract them. Also, the ghost who attacked me hurt a girl who happened to walk by while he was strangling me—she had no idea what was going on. I guess she thought I had had a seizure. She tried to help, and he threw her against a tree. Knocked her out cold and broke her collarbone." That had been the second time, though Josie kept that little fact to herself. She took a deep breath, old guilt slithering through her. "I can't risk that happening to people I love."

"Jeez, Josie." Bryce was quiet for so long she almost gave up on further conversation. "I misjudged you."

She squirmed. "You didn't know."

"I should've asked. We were friends once." Self-recrimination in his tones only made the guilt worse.

"Telling you wasn't an option."

"I would've believed you eventually."

Her lips hitched in a sad smile. One he couldn't see. "Maybe."

He put his forehead to the back of her head, pulling her in tighter. This might be heaven, or hell. Maybe they'd fallen off that cliff too, instead of rescuing Peter.

"But that was a few years ago," he murmured, almost to himself, as if he was working things out. "You only moved home and started living alone last year."

She squirmed again and didn't say anything, holding her breath that he didn't ask if she'd been hurt again.

"Aren't you lonely?" A barely-there brush of his fingers against her skin gained her full attention. She held her breath and her body still. Had he meant to do that? Or was he just teasing her?

She twisted her lips. "Sometimes."

"Do you remember fishing with me?" And there it was again. The whisper of a touch. That combined with his question had her stomach clenching in response.

Josie cleared her suddenly parched throat. Where had she put the water? "Yes."

"I kissed you goodbye."

Why bring this up now? She scrunched her eyes closed.

"I remember." No other kiss before that had come close. She suspected none ever would, not that she saw a future in which she'd get to find out.

"I wish I'd spent more time kissing you." His voice thickened, and now the actions of his fingers against her skin became deliberate as he traced a lazy pattern over her taut belly.

"Oh." She squeaked the word out and tried to calm her racing heart. "I guess we all have regrets." Like having to push him away when she returned home, as she did with her family. She had no choice.

"I guess so." His fingers kept up the dance across her skin and an answering ache bloomed deep inside her.

"Josie?" He whispered her name. A caress of sound, his voice husky.

"Yeah?"

"I want to kiss you now."

CHAPTER 7

BRYCE HELD his breath and waited for Josie's response, although he didn't stop touching her. Couldn't. Warm and soft and silky beneath his fingertips, he wanted more. So much more.

Please say yes.

Josie turned in his arms to face him, dislodging his hand. Her face remained hidden in the pitch black, but her warm breath tickled his chin. "I…" She paused, almost seeming to hold her breath. "I guess you'd better kiss me, then."

Thank God.

Bryce didn't need to be asked twice, lowering his head in a rush, only to bump her cheek with his nose. "Ouch."

Josie giggled. A sound he hadn't heard from her in years. Sexiest damn noise ever.

"Let's try that again." Angling his head based on the first try, he found her lips. Deliberately, he leashed the urgency riding him, to offer her something gentle. Reverent.

She tasted like toothpaste and sweetness. Not that he would admit it to himself this past year or so, but he had craved this since the last time.

She pulled away slightly, breathless. "If you're going to kiss me, don't hold back."

With a half-laugh, half-groan, he deepened the kiss. Long denied desire combined with the frantic day, and the new discoveries about her. About himself too. He couldn't hold back anymore if he wanted to. While plumbing the secret depths of her mouth and tangling his tongue with hers, he trailed his left hand up her thigh, over her hip, and searched for the swath of skin at her waist, which had tormented him while they talked.

Ah, there. She shuddered under the contact.

"Too cold?" he asked against her lips.

"No," she whispered, before resuming the kiss. She caught his lower lip between her teeth and desire zinged all the way through his body.

He jerked back, breathing hard. "Too fast. Too soon."

She shook her head, trying to tug him closer. "Not soon enough."

He knew what she meant. Still, he held strong. "We've had so many misunderstandings. We should take this slow. Get to know each other again."

She froze beneath him, the puffs of their heavy breathing the only sound in the tent. Her stillness was a warning.

"We can't."

"Can't what?"

"Get to know each other again. We can't be friends...or lovers beyond tonight."

What the hell?

Without moving away from her, he fumbled for the lantern and turned on the light with a flick. He needed to see her face for this. "I'm not having a one-night-stand with you."

"Fine." She'd shut him out. Again. Her face was a total blank.

Impotent anger beat against his insides, battering them like a storm raged at the mountains. "That's it? Fine?"

Her gaze hardened. "Yeah. Fine. You won't do just tonight. I can't do a future."

"Why?"

A little wrinkle appeared between her eyebrows. "I guess we're at an impasse."

He ran a hand through his hair needing some outlet for the anger building in him. "This makes no damn sense. Why can't you do a future?"

Now her gaze skittered away. "My situation hasn't changed."

Her situation? What was she talking about? He searched her face, mouth tight, jaw strained, and realization dawned. "You mean with the ghosts?"

She shrugged.

He could handle ghosts...couldn't he? Cold creeped over him, seeping into his bones, settling in with realization. She'd shut out her entire family. To protect them, he got that. Which meant she protected him now. Maybe she always had.

The memory of the bruises—ugly and black around her neck—rose inside him like a spirit of the past. A ghost had done that to her? No wonder she was hiding.

How did he maneuver around a limitation like that? He needed time to think. But, how did they move forward if she couldn't? Or wouldn't?

Bryce let loose a long exhale. "Okay."

Josie relaxed beneath him. She turned her head and searched his eyes. "You're not mad?"

He brushed a strand of hair from her face with fingers that shook. "Disappointed, yes." Determined to fix this somehow. "But no, not mad."

Not now that he understood her reasons.

Her lips twisted. Were those tears she blinked away? "Good."

Where did he go from there? "I guess we should get some sleep."

In answer she rolled away from him as much as the constriction of the sleeping bag allowed, and he turned the light off. "Night, Bryce."

"Goodnight."

CHAPTER 8

Josie walked around the large stone fireplace that was the centerpiece of her home, into her tiny but functional kitchen and came to a screeching halt. In the middle of the room stood two apparitions, pale imitations of their former selves. Some ghosts floated, some flew, some acted as they did when they were alive, walking around like people. These two stood and stared.

She gaped at them before her manners kicked in. "Mr. and Mrs. Evans. It's nice to see you again."

Bryce's mom gave her a warm smile while his dad nodded.

"It's been a while," she added politely, hiding a grimace.

"You've kept us away," Bill Evans said. No accusation in his voice though. "When you moved home, after the attack, we tried to contact you, but an invisible wall we couldn't get through—coming from you—kept us away."

Wait... Was that why she hadn't seen ghosts since coming home? She assumed avoiding her family, and any places where spirits regularly lingered, had kept them away. Had she been keeping them away herself? How? "But you're here now?"

"When Peter broke through, we followed."

Which meant others could, too? Terror raked a claw down her spine. Not good. Still, she loved the two people standing before her. "I've missed you."

"We've missed you too, honey," Joyce Evans said, her see through face both sad and smiling, cracking Josie's heart like ice breaking open a boulder.

She shifted on her feet. "As lovely as it is to see you, um… any particular reason for the visit?"

Joyce gave her a soft smile. "Bryce is at the door. You should let him in. Talk to him."

With a happy chime, the doorbell rang, and they vanished, fading into oblivion. Josie stared at the empty space. Shock warring with anticipation paralyzed her. The second peel of the bell got her moving.

She cracked open the door. "Bryce?"

He scanned her face, expression serious. "Hi."

She raised her eyebrows. What was he doing here?

"May I come in?"

Josie hesitated. Bryce had never visited her home before. Not this one. The house was small, but homey, with a cozy living space and kitchen downstairs, separated by the fireplace, which looked through to both sides. Her loft bedroom and bathroom were upstairs, sporting spectacular views of the mountains through floor-to-ceiling windows. But what would Bryce think? He built new million-dollar mountain cabins for the rich and famous.

She sighed and swung the door open. "Sure."

He paused just inside, his gaze taking in the surroundings. "I love old cabins like these. The new ones are pretty, but these feel like…"

"Home?" She shouldn't be surprised that was how he felt.

He glanced down at her, a small smile playing around his mouth. "Yeah."

Dangerous to let him into her heart. Even in small ways. "I've always thought so." She led the way to the kitchen. "Can I get you a drink? Water? Soda?"

"No, thanks."

He snagged a stool at the kitchen counter, sat, and waited while she poured herself a glass of water. The action was more to keep her hands occupied than anything.

"So…" She turned to face him. "Why are you here?"

"Checking on you. I wanted to make sure you're okay."

The morning after the rescue, Jared had radioed up, letting them know Peter's surgery had been successful and he was awake. And Josie could breathe again. That Swiss cheese incident had scared the shit out of her.

They'd hiked back down and gone their separate ways. Was it only yesterday? Now she was clean, dressed in her favorite comfy jeans paired with a black tank top and a loose white sweater…and Bryce's gaze kept drifting to her cleavage, a heat in those dark depths that she hadn't thought she'd ever see. She didn't have the right to wish for it now. Even so, an answering warmth bloomed inside her, tried to loosen her muscles and her resolve.

She needed to get him out of here. Now.

She circled the rim of her water glass with her fingertip. "I'm fine. Especially because Peter will be okay."

Bryce nodded. "Good. Have you seen him yet?"

She scrunched up her face. "No. Maybe tonight." Hospitals were off limits to her—guaranteed hauntings—but she could video phone him.

"Seen anymore ghosts lately?"

"I have." Suddenly, she had the oddest urge to be fully transparent with Bryce.

Maybe because now she didn't have to hide who and

what she was. Maybe because he made her feel safe. Protected. Or maybe the seduction of sharing her life with this man became too much to resist. Plus, the ghosts who'd visited her linked directly to him.

She wasn't quite sure how to ease into this. "Your parents were here."

He straightened in his chair and he looked around as though he might see them any second. "They were?"

"A few minutes before you showed up. They told me to let you in."

Shock filled his eyes even as an affectionate smile graced his lips. "I'll be damned." He looked at her. "I got the impression you didn't see them anymore."

"I hadn't for quite a while until today."

Concern tugged at the corners of his mouth. "Are they stuck? Why aren't they in heaven?"

Without consciously deciding to, she reached across the counter for his hand. "It's not like that. Some spirits are stuck, as you imagine. The good ones find spirit talkers, like me, to help them resolve something left undone. But many just come for a visit, to check on loved ones. Like your parents. They've checked on you repeatedly since their death, popping in to say hi to me and brag about you when they did."

Until the last year at least.

"But you haven't seen them in a while?" He turned his hand and laced their fingers together. Her stomach dipped at the more intimate contact. She wanted to pull back. She should pull back. But she didn't.

"They said I'd blocked them out since...the attack."

"Oh."

She wanted to hold hands like this for hours, and that realization finally made her pull away, her skin tingling at the loss of contact. She took a quick sip of water for something to do. "Thanks for coming by, Bryce. I appreciate it."

He leaned back in his chair. "I make a mean spaghetti."

She paused, mouth wide open. "Um…Good for you?"

"Maybe you could come over tonight and give me your opinion?"

He was asking her on a date? After everything? The urge to say yes pressed in on her, lifted her higher and she was tempted. Almost. However, knowing the hole his parents had come through existed in whatever wall she'd built up over the years had her worried. What else could come through? "I'm more of a meat and potatoes girl."

Bryce's expression shifted subtly, becoming both more intense and more…tender? The expression reaching inside her to surround her heart. *God this was so hard.*

"I can't. You know that."

He got up from his seat and stalked around the island toward her, not stopping when he hit her personal boundaries, backing Josie up until she hit the counter. Dark eyes, completely focused on her, bore through all the walls she was trying to slam up between them. "I'm not going to give up now that I know what's keeping you apart." His lips quirked. "How about you save us some time, and just let me in?"

Yes trembled on her lips, in the need arching through her body at his nearness and his words. But her mind recoiled in fear. *If he gets hurt, it's all my fault.*

Her alarm drove her to be harsh. "You forgot all about me once. It shouldn't be hard to do it again."

Rather than get angry back, or leave, or offer any other easy response, he gently tucked a strand of hair behind her ear. "You're not going to get rid of me that easily this time."

She licked suddenly dry lips, resisting the urge to lean into his touch.

"Do you know what the wait for you has been?" he asked.

She shook her head.

"Foreplay."

She tried to deny it, reject the notion, but the only noise she could produce was a squeak.

"And torture." He grinned, devilry dancing in his eyes.

Oh jeez.

"I..." she paused and swallowed. The way he was looking at her was every fantasy rolled into a moment of sheer wanting. Tender and hot and compelling and....

With a tiny noise at the back of her throat, Josie was in his arms. This wasn't like that kiss that hot summer night. That had been sweet and slow. Tentative even as they'd carefully felt their way across the boundary of friendship. But this was heated. And frantic.

Bryce was right. All the denial had been foreplay.

A building of tension like a tea kettle. His lips on hers only ratcheted her need to an entirely unfamiliar level. Both familiar like coming home and enticingly new.

Dangerous.

Josie pulled away, breathing hard. "Nothing has changed."

"Uh-huh." His lips were back on hers, and God forgive her she didn't want to stop.

But she made herself try one more time. "If anything ever happened to you because of me—"

In answer Bryce picked her up in his arms and walked toward the back of her house where her room was. The take charge part of him taking charge. Damn if she didn't want to give in and just let him take control.

He kicked the door open, but then paused, looking down into her eyes in the sweetest way before he gently laid her on the bed. Only instead of claiming her mouth, he braced his hands on the bed on either side of her face. "I know you're scared."

"Everything has changed."

"Exactly."

She made a sound of frustration at the back of her throat, but he only grinned. "I tell you what… This—right here and now—is for us. Because we both need this. No strings or expectations. We'll figure out what it means or where we go next later. But," He closed his eyes and shook his head, tension riding his shoulders. "Please, Josie, don't turn me away now."

Right now, was all she could offer. Heart cracking wide open with the knowledge that this was it, Josie knew she couldn't walk away. If this was all they had, she'd hold on with both hands. Just for a second.

Slowly, she raised up on her elbows and, holding Bryce's watchful gaze, softly kissed him.

"Thank God," he groaned against her, then took over.

In a rush, the frantic need returned and, hands fumbling between rough kisses, they stripped each other bare. As soon as she was free of her clothes, Bryce's mouth was on her, hands kneading and molding, and each touch, each brush of those talented fingers, each lave of his tongue and she fell deeper into a haze of sensual need.

Nothing like she'd ever experienced before. Because this was Bryce, and her heart was just as invested as her body in sharing this moment with him.

Always had been.

While he explored every inch of her, she obsessively, shamelessly did the same to him. The man was incredible— all that outdoorsing and carpentry had given some of his muscles their own muscles. Overwhelmed by everything, she buried her face in the crook of his neck, enjoying the woodsy scent of him, wanting to absorb him, absorb every piece of magic in this moment so that she could remember.

Desperation clawing at her to remember it all.

She snaked her hand between them, and wrapped it

around his hot, straining shaft, and Bryce grunted. With a smile, she squeezed and pumped, only twice, and then his hand was over hers.

"Keep that up, and I'm not sure how long I'll last," he murmured, laughter in his voice. But then he sobered, looking her in the eyes. "I've waited so long, fantasized about this for so long..."

"I know," she whispered.

The tempo of their touches changed, gentled, turned to an exploration that was still desperate, but also so much more.

She was writhing beneath his touch by the time he positioned himself at her entrance. The pause lengthened and she opened slumberous eyes.

"What?"

"Condom."

She smiled. "I'm on the pill, and I'm clean."

A breath of relief punched from him. "Good. I'm clean too."

Gently, excruciatingly slowly, he threaded their fingers together, raising her hands to lie on either side of her face on the bed, then, staring deeply into her eyes, he pushed inside. Slowly. So achingly slowly, until he'd filled her up with every inch of him.

Bryce grunted, the sound almost pained. "You're the most beautiful thing I've ever seen," he whispered. "I wish..."

Her heart contracted and then expanded in a single rush of waiting and wanting. Only he shook his head, then slid out as slowly as he'd entered her and slid back in.

Staring at each other, as though neither of them wanted to miss a single second, Bryce gradually increased the pace, building the pressure, the heat, the need swelling and flowing inside her, pushed higher by the connection.

Whimpers tumbled from her lips, but she didn't look

away. And then that pressure turned to tingling, gathering at the base of her spine.

"Bryce?" she whispered.

"I'm right there with you, Josie," he said. "Let go."

Her orgasm came in a rush of sensation, like white water slamming through her and tossing her. Only Bryce's eyes anchored her to him through the tumult as he shouted his own completion.

Gradually he slowed as the rush ebbed, their bodies turning languorous in the aftermath of something so beautiful, she felt filled up. Body and soul.

Perfect.

Bryce gathered her in his arms, pulling her into his body, his breathing easing with her own. "I always knew it would be that way for us," he murmured as he nuzzled her temple.

Josie closed her eyes tight against the urge to turn into him, to pretend that they could have more.

Silence filled the room, filled the man next to her, and she could feel him watching her. Then he let loose a long breath. "It's okay, Josie. I can already see you worrying."

Missing him before he'd gone, actually. But she didn't say that.

Instead she turned her head and opened her eyes to face him. "I—"

He silenced her with a kiss. "Don't say it. I already know." Then he levered off the bed and started to pull on his pants.

Josie raised up onto her elbows, careful to keep the sheets around her body. "What does that mean?"

She needed to be sure that he understood. That she couldn't put him at risk with more. That blue-eyed devil was still out there. She didn't know what held him back, why he didn't just come for her, or why there were gaps of time between attacks. But he was going after her loved ones now.

"It means I know why you're scared. I know why you're

pushing me away. I don't have answers…yet." Fully dressed, he moved to the side of the bed and leaned over her. "But I'm not giving up that we'll find one."

"What if we never do?" she whispered. Didn't he think she'd tried? She'd researched all she could find. Talked with her family.

Bryce grimaced. "I don't know."

At least he was being honest.

He leaned down and kissed her softly. "See you later."

Not until she figured this out, he wouldn't. He walked to the door, then paused and looked back at her "If you see them again, tell my parents… Tell them I miss them."

The door shut behind him with a soft click followed by the usual loud bang of her front door. Josie winced. *Really need to get that fixed.*

Hell, her entire life needed to get fixed.

She blew out a pent-up breath. Bryce still had hope, but she knew better. They weren't going to get any answers. He needed to move on with his life. Love someone else.

He'd figure that out eventually. Just as she had.

CHAPTER 9

Josie hated hospitals. So many ghosts hung out in those places, they were as bad as graveyards, old hotels, and, strangely, bars. She avoided all those places as if the zombie apocalypse had started there already. Except Pete was in one now, and she wanted to see him alive and solidly human with her own eyes. The video call hadn't cut it.

Courage was currently taking the form of a lump in her throat that she tried to swallow around as she pushed through the turnstile glass doors into the cool, institutional hospital foyer. The smell of antiseptic and death, never pleasant, made her nose twitch.

A quick check with the nurse at the front desk gave her directions to Peter's room. She knocked softly on the door before cracking it open and sticking her head inside. Peter lay in the dimly lit room with his leg suspended above the bed by what appeared to be a medieval torture device disguised as modern by the white and chrome of it. The head of the bed was propped up, and he sat there with the remote in his hand, staring blankly at a TV playing old 90s reruns.

"Hey," she called softly.

He glanced over and grinned. "Never expected to find you in a hospital unless death was imminent."

"Yours or mine?"

He shrugged. "Toss up."

Josie dragged a chair, screeching across the tiles, from the wall to his bedside and sat. "How are you?"

"I'll live. Because of you."

She cocked her head. "Do you remember anything?"

"Complete blank. Mom told me you and Bryce found me, but how? I went off trail. How did you know?"

She grimaced. "You kind of appeared to me."

"You're kidding!" He jerked forward, only to flop back against the bed with a groan and clutched at his suspended leg. Sweat popped out over his brow.

Josie ached for him, completely helpless as she watched him struggle through the pain. Healing would be a much better superpower.

"What's the diagnosis?" she asked when he finally relaxed.

"Snapped my femur in half and barely missed severing the artery. Luckily no bone fragments are floating around in there that they can detect. The doctors determined I need more surgery in a few days, hence the traction. About five or six months of recovery ahead of me."

"But at least you *get* to recover."

He turned his head to regard her seriously, very un-Peter-like. "Thanks to you… I really appeared to you?"

She shrugged and indicated the bed. "You're here now, aren't you?"

"That's right." Peter's gaze went hazy, as though he was looking at something else. "I remember now. I followed a ghost I saw. He had the creepiest blue eyes."

No. Josie froze, every part of her focused on her brother's words. *It couldn't be.*

But there was only one ghost she'd ever seen with eyes

like that. The coincidence was too great. Panic choked her, threatening to steal her breath. She needed to get out of here. Quickly. Before Peter guessed or saw her distress.

She cleared her throat. "I guess you followed the ghost over a cliff. Next thing I know, you're standing in my kitchen in see-through form." She managed to lift one eyebrow, sending her brother an irritated look. "Please don't ever do that again."

"I'll try." His easy grin was back, and Josie rolled her eyes.

"How'd Bryce get in on it?" he asked.

"You forced me to ask him for help. You led us to your body."

Breathing was still difficult around lungs that didn't want to function. At least Peter didn't appear to notice her distress. "Sounds gruesome. How'd you explain having to go off trail to Bryce?"

She scrunched up her nose. "He knows about our family secret now."

He pleated the white sheet covering all but his suspended leg as he thought that through. "About time, I guess."

"I agree." Bryce said from the doorway.

Josie jerked her gaze to him with a gasp. He'd changed from the slacks and button down he'd worn to her house this morning into jeans and a hockey t-shirt which emphasized his muscles even more. Had he dressed up for her earlier?

A buzz of reaction kick-started her lungs again, the memory of how he'd touched her, how he'd felt inside her, and especially how he'd watched her so tenderly as they both reached that perfect pleasure in each other. Only what Peter said clamped back down on them as she stared at the man she'd been in love with her entire life.

If that blue-eyed bastard came near him—

"Hey buddy!" Peter grinned. He glanced between them. "You two come together?"

"No. Just a pleasant coincidence." The look Bryce cast Josie's way sent a shiver of anticipation cascading down her spine, even though she'd already said they could only have the one time. How the heck did he do that?

His arrival was as good an excuse to leave as any. "I'd better go. Let you two catch up." She squeezed Peter's hand. "He can fill you in on the details."

"Don't go because of me," Bryce said.

"It's okay," Peter said. "Hospitals aren't great for people like us. Especially Josie."

"I see. Makes sense. Lots of deaths."

Josie rose from her seat and leaned in to give Peter a careful hug. "I'll see you later."

"Love you."

"Back atchya."

She skirted Bryce to get to the door, only he stepped into her space, crowding her with his size and sex appeal. Damn he smelled good.

"See you later, Josie," he murmured, his low voice rasping along her nerve endings in an annoyingly tempting way.

She scooted around him and out the door with more haste than grace. Trying to hustle out of the building, she kept her eyes forward though she didn't encounter any spirits as she went. Josie almost made it to the front door when she came to a screeching halt. The blood slowed in her veins, and then her heart double pumped as terror grabbed hold with icy hands straight from the grave.

"You," she whispered.

A man hovered before her, a blue specter. In his human life he had been tall, well over six feet, with dark hair. Hard to tell what color his eyes were. They glowed an eerie blue now, almost silver, the intensity so blinding.

The apparition opened its mouth in a grin. A shivery sensation akin to electricity bolted down her spine.

"I knew if I went after your family, you'd come out of hiding," he said with a sneer.

BRYCE ROUNDED the corner of the sterile hospital corridor, all whites and greys with fluorescent lighting buzzing overhead. He slowed as he caught sight of Josie—hard to miss those gorgeous sandy-colored curls. She stood in front of the exit, her back rigid, fists clenched at her sides. She'd left him and Peter as if her pretty shoes were on fire at least fifteen minutes ago. Had she been standing here the entire time?

He approached her from the side, not wanting to startle her. "Josie?"

"Don't." She shot out a hand, palm up toward him, a clear signal to stop. Lips flat and face pale, she half-whispered, half-choked the word.

"What?"

She didn't look at him. "Walk away." Now she was whispering.

"What's wrong?"

"Please go."

Her gaze remained locked on something in front of her. Something he couldn't see. Was there a ghost there?

"I'm not—"

"Go!" she snapped. The command seemed driven more by fear than anger.

Bryce's heart clenched inside him, his hands fisting at his side. He hated seeing her terrified, hated even more how impotent he was in this moment. Carefully, he held up his hands and backed away. "Okay."

He took two steps in the direction she continued to stare, when she gasped and reached for him. "Stop!"

Bryce clenched his jaw. "You just told me to go."

"Not you," she hissed.

Yanking Bryce aside, she bodily put herself in front of him. "Please stop."

Although she appeared to be pleading with the door, all Bryce's warning bells went off. Instinctively, he kept quiet.

"No." Josie paused as if listening and then backed up a step, practically shoving him along with her. "No. Dammit."

She shook so badly, it vibrated through the grip she had on him. She shuffled back again. Then one more time. Her body went rigid a split second before she turned and shoved him to the floor, dropping down over him, one arm raised to ward off whatever was terrorizing her, the other arm draped protectively over him.

A zap like an electric shock sizzled through her to him. Then...nothing.

Except for the sound of Josie's harsh breathing—so fast she was close to hyperventilating. After a long beat, she raised her head, searching around them. Her shoulders dropped a fraction as her wild gaze sought his.

Then she dropped her forehead to his chest, breath coming in harsh rasps. "He's gone."

CHAPTER 10

Josie rose to her feet, shaking and utterly disoriented, and pulled her sweater up over her shoulder where it had slipped off in her frantic bid to protect Bryce.

What just happened? The last time she encountered this spirit, he'd tried to choke her to death for a second time and thrown a girl against a tree. Only, the way he'd been talking…

He'd said something about needing her body. But why kill her? Or had he just been trying to subdue her in order to possess her? She had suspected the thing had led Peter off the edge of the mountain in a bid to get to her, maybe draw her out of hiding. Now she knew for sure.

Today he came at her and Bryce as though he planned to do more bodily harm, only to disappear with a shriek followed by screaming silence that had echoed all around her.

"Josie?"

In a daze she turned to face Bryce. "I…have to go." Before he could respond, she took off, pushing through the revolving door and into the brisk night air. She had to find out what was going on. She could think of only one place to get answers quickly where she wouldn't look like a total lunatic.

"Hold up." Bryce caught up to her outside the doors and snagged her by the arm.

"I need to be somewhere." She pulled out of his grip and continued walking.

He kept pace. "Where?"

She stayed quiet.

"Josie, talk to me."

She paused at the door to her SUV, keys in hand, and allowed his concern…and his strength…to wash over her. Bryce had been a friend once, her girlhood protector. She'd relied on him for advice or to be an ear when she needed to vent. She hadn't realized exactly how much she'd missed him until all this. Worse, especially, right now, when she felt so alone.

"Get in." She waved at the SUV.

Barely aware of her actions, she unlocked the doors. They both hopped in, and she revved the engine and put it in gear.

"Where are we going?"

"The graveyard."

Silence greeted that statement. She glanced over to find him studying her, concern etched in the brackets around his mouth.

Sigh. "I told you about the ghost who attacked me?"

"Yes."

"That was him. Only last time he put me *and* another girl in the hospital. A few weeks before you surprised me with that visit. And I'm pretty sure he's the one Peter saw on the mountain. But this time…" She shook her head, going over every detail in her mind. What the hell had happened?

"This time…?"

"He disappeared just as he seemed about to attack."

"Why?"

"No clue. That's why the graveyard. I'm hoping to get answers there."

"Good place for ghosts." He was quick on the uptake.

"And, unlike the hospital, isolated, so no living people to see me chatting to thin air. When we get there, you need to stay in the truck."

"No way. I'm not letting you do this on your own."

She made a scoffing noise at the back of her throat. "I'll be fine."

"I know you will, but I still want to be there for you."

Don't cry. Don't cry. Don't cry. Her new mantra these days, apparently. She'd shut out everyone she loved to protect them, but now this fucker was going after those same people. And it had seen Bryce, seen her protect Bryce.

God. If anything happened to him because of her... "I can't let you. What if he shows up again?"

"It's my choice to take that risk. Not yours."

"Stubborn man," she muttered.

"When it concerns you? Absolutely."

"Why?"

From the corner of her eye, she caught the way he stiffened in his seat.

"What do you mean why?" he asked.

"After a year of hardly a word... You'd moved on. I know you had. So...why?"

"Do you know why I was so awkward with you all this time?"

She scowled. Was he avoiding the topic? "Because you thought I was being a jerk to my family."

"No. I was *worried* about you. But mostly...I'd fallen in love with you...had been in love with you for years."

Holy crap.

Her heart tried its best to charge right out of her body, only contained by her ribs.

"After that kiss that summer, I hoped…" He stared out the front windshield to the ribbon of road illuminated by the headlights, though she wasn't sure if he saw anything. "Then you shut me out. Shut everyone out."

He turned in the seat to face her, determination written in the hard line of his jaw, his lips, his eyes. "Now I know why, I'm not letting you shut me out anymore. I meant it when I said we'd find answers. Figure this out. Because I can't lose you again, Josie."

She had no clue what to say, so she kept her eyes on the road. Neither of them spoke again, both lost in their own thoughts, until she parked along the road next to the grave-yard and turned off the engine.

After undoing her seatbelt, Josie faced the man she'd crushed on as a teen, loved from afar through the last year, and fallen in love with all over again tonight. "You don't want me to shut you out."

He studied her face, his intense gaze trailing across her features. "No."

"And I can't watch you get hurt, maybe die, because of me." Courage pulsed through her, and her heart leapt into her throat. She leaned across the space between them and took Bryce's face in her hands. She laid a long, sweet kiss on his lips, then pulled back with reluctance. "I protect those I love. Please stay here."

In answer he groaned and surged forward to take her lips in a searing kiss. The familiar heat pooled low, radiating throughout her body until her toes curled, and she chased his touch as he sat back.

He hit her with a cheeky grin. "No damn way."

CHAPTER 11

A WISPY MIST swirled around the wrought iron gates leading into the graveyard that had been part of the town since the 1800s and continued to meander among the headstones. Most people would be creeped out here at night, but not Josie. At least...not when the ghosts were nice. She hadn't been in a graveyard since the attack, avoiding any locations where spirits hung out in number. Before, she had always found this spot peaceful, a place to get advice from those older and wiser than she.

However, tonight, instead of finding spirits waiting or appearing as she walked among them, the stones greeted her with cold, blank silence.

She'd been so sure.

"What's wrong?" Bryce stayed by her side, a silent shadow.

She shifted on her feet. "No one's showing up."

"Is that normal?"

"No." She chewed at her bottom lip.

"You have to let us in, Josie." She jerked as the whispered words reached her ears.

"How?" she called out. No answer came.

A swift glance at Bryce showed him watching intently. "They say I have to let them in."

"How do you do that?"

"Good question," she muttered.

Josie shifted on her feet again, dithering. How did one go about letting ghosts in? They used to just show up. Her gaze trailed to the man at her side. The man she'd shut out. Had she ruined any chance for them? Had she shut out the ghosts the same way? How did you let someone in again?

Beside her, Bryce cautiously surveyed the grounds, as though a ghost might pop up in front of him any second.

"Bryce?" she asked.

He turned to face her, eyebrows raised.

Certainty blazed inside her heart. You let someone in by taking the first step toward them. But did she have the courage to take the risk? "I have to ask you a question."

"What?" His voice had dropped, rumbling around Josie in the quiet of the graveyard, giving her an added boost of confidence.

She sucked in a deep breath and plunged in headfirst. "I've loved you since I was twelve and you made Peter stop hitting me with snowballs."

Bryce's lips hitched, but he gave no other reaction.

Josie forged ahead, determined to finish this. "As I grew older, my crush changed, grew. I had to push you away to protect you from the danger I attracted, but I've always known how amazing you are—smart, loyal, trustworthy. I may have stopped spending time with you, but I never stopped caring." Her voice cracked and she dropped her gaze to the ground as she struggled for control.

Two feet appeared in her line of vision before two warm hands took hers in their grip, giving her the strength she needed to keep going. She lifted her gaze to his eyes and gasped. Everything she'd ever wanted looked back at her from his deep brown eyes—love, acceptance, desire, need.

A smile trembled on her lips. "I'm ready to take a chance now. Stop shutting you out. If you want me."

Bryce jerked her into his arms. "If I want you?" He buried his face in her hair. "I think I never got serious about anyone else because I've been waiting for you."

Pure happiness warmed her body from her heart outward, like a spring thaw as the sun hit the frost, turning it silver. "So, you love me too?"

"Yes, I do." He tugged her flush up against his body and lowered his lips to hers, kissing her with the enthusiasm of a thirsty man who had finally found a river of pure clear water. Lips and tongue played with hers, teeth nipping at her bottom lip. Her heart tripped along on a happy pitter-patter, as a feeling of rightness entwined with the exhilaration of pounding desire.

"How sweet," a familiar voice hissed.

Josie jerked her head around to find the specter there. Again. She shouldn't be surprised. He followed her everywhere it seemed, and she was surrounded by spirits here.

Fear turned her blood to sludge in her veins, her heart having to pump double time to force it through.

"What do you want?" Damn the shake to her voice.

"You."

Josie tried to stand her ground, except her legs were shaking so hard they might fail her at any second. "Why me?"

"If you're this powerful, I can take over your body—you would survive a long-term possession nicely, unlike most humans. Believe me I've tried. Then I can get on with living my own life." His almost translucent eyes seemed to shift to Bryce. "And no one else can have you. Not if I want my possession to take."

"It's okay, Josie." Bryce's mother's voice whispered beside her. "We're here. And you are strong. So strong."

The trembling in her legs eased up. *I'm not alone.*

"Get behind me," she said to Bryce without turning her head. "If I move, move with me, stay at my back. Got it?"

He said nothing. Just stepped behind her, close enough she could feel his heat. Strong hands settled at her hips, and somehow that small connection was all she needed.

She wasn't alone in so many ways.

"Cute," the specter sneered. "It's not going to help you."

"But we will," Bryce's dad suddenly appeared at her other side. Along with a man she didn't recognize.

"All of us," another voice said.

Josie sucked in, almost choking on her own shock. Lined up to either side of her, more spirits than she could count, forming a wall with her.

The specter opened his mouth in a gaping, horrifying act of a scream, and total silence. Then he shot forward, coming for her, and the scream whistled behind him.

The ghosts standing with her moved at the same time, a cacophony of yells that would terrify a lesser mortal ripped from their throats as they swarmed him, dragging him down to the ground, piling on top of him to hold him there.

"Josie. Now," Bryce's dad yelled.

And somehow, she knew exactly what to do.

"Stay here," she said to Bryce. Then she stepped forward.

Unafraid, she waded through the spirits forms, like pushing into the waves of the ocean. He glared at her from cold, dead eyes that set a hard chill in her bones. But the flicker of fear there gave her the determination she needed. Around all these ghosts she could feel her power inside herself. Like the buzz of electrical wires. She pictured that electric current traveling along her nerve endings and in her blood. Not entirely knowing how, she gathered that power, pulling it outside her body until her hands started to glow and heat, electric lines wrapping around them in snaking, sizzling strands. In a sharp, sudden move, she placed both her hands on top of her own personal haunting's head. But instead of passing through, she hit a solid surface. Immediately, his form lit up as her power surged into him, his form glowing bright blue as electricity rippled over him and through him and within him.

"Holy shit," Bryce muttered behind her.

He could see this?

Again, the man opened his mouth in that terrifying silent scream, but she held on. Seconds later a high-pitched sound, like the whistle of a kettle and the scream of true evil all in one, split the night air, echoing throughout the graveyard.

Under her palm, he started to jerk and writhe, then his body started to disintegrate. Ragged holes appeared all over him, like a moth-eaten blanket, growing larger. The screams and his thrashing turned more violent, but her ghosts held on and so did Josie, until the holes of nothing consumed him. As the last of him disappeared, the sound cut off abruptly, leaving a gaping silence in its wake.

Breathing hard, Josie pitched forward, hands to her knees. What the hell had just happened?

"Thank you," she whispered to the ghosts all around her.

With smiles and murmurs, they slowly faded away.

"Josie?"

Bryce's voice was directly behind her. With a frantic noise at the back of her throat, she spun and threw herself into his arms. "He's gone," she whispered.

"I know." He slid a hand over the back of her head in a comforting gesture. "You don't have to be afraid anymore."

Oh my God. I don't. She closed her eyes, clinging tighter to the man she'd loved since she was old enough to know what that meant.

Leaning back, she smiled up at him, letting her gaze roam freely over his features. She was free. Free to live her life. Free to love this man.

As though he heard her thoughts, Bryce grinned and kissed her hard.

"About time!" a deep voice interrupted.

Bryce leapt from her at the sound of his father's voice. Though he kept a hand on her arm, he whirled to the source.

"Dad?" His voice broke.

Bryce's mother hovered beside her husband. "Can you see us?" she asked Bryce.

He nodded slowly, before glancing Josie's way. "Is that normal?"

She shrugged. "Not really."

He turned back to his parents. "It's…" He took a shuddering breath, looking about as shaken as she'd ever seen him. Then he smiled. "Oh, God, it's good to see you."

His parents smiled in return, their delight radiant even through their transparency. "We've been close by, watching. We're so proud of the man you've become."

Bryce swallowed hard. "I've missed you."

Another smile from both parents. Sadder. Harder to see.

"We've missed you, too. But now we can rest, knowing you'll be all right." Bryce's dad tipped his head in Josie's direction.

Her jaw dropped. "You knew?"

His mother's laugh tinkled over the space between them, filling the somber place with joy. "He's been in love with you since you were kids. You're meant to be together."

Tears burned at the back of her eyes. "What just happened?"

"After keeping us all out, you can block out any ghosts at will. Even ones like that." Bryce's mom scowled briefly before her expression cleared. "And tonight, your love for Bryce unlocked you in some instinctual way. Like letting yourself feel everything you could for him also allowed you to feel your powers."

That was how it had felt. She had no idea if she could do it again. But she was willing to have faith.

"That ghost is gone forever," Joyce said.

"Where?"

They shook their heads, and somehow Josie didn't want to know.

Except she didn't know how she was doing it. What if her protections failed her? "How do I know I can do it again?"

Bill's gaze held the wisdom of the ages. "You don't, but I have confidence."

Josie bit her lip. She'd already taken one leap of faith tonight. Could she believe they were right? Was it possible she possessed the ability to hold off any malevolent spirit who wished Josie or her loved ones harm? Perhaps belief was the key. Could she believe?

Bryce's hand crept into hers, lacing their fingers together, palm to palm.

Damn straight she could.

Excitement bubbled up inside. She bounced on her toes, unable to contain the pent-up energy fizzing through her. All that solitude. Time wasted. At least it was over.

Bryce squeezed her hand. "You don't have to hide anymore. Or be alone."

He voiced her thoughts exactly. "I know."

He pulled her into his arms. "You'll never get rid of me now."

She huffed a laugh into his shoulder. "Isn't that my line?"

He glanced over the top of her head to his parents. "Wait…"

Josie turned to find they were fading. "Thank you," she mouthed.

"We'll always be watching," His father assured them both.

"We love you." The echo of his mother's words lingered in the mist as they disappeared.

"I love you too," Bryce called after them. "Always."

Josie smiled softly. "They heard you. I'm sure they'll be back."

EPILOGUE

THE WAIL of her infant son pulled Josie from sleep—again. She groaned. Not yet. She had just got him down an hour ago after being up half the night. Given that they had plans to go to her family's for Thanksgiving today, more sleep than that would have been nice.

Bryce rolled over and planted a kiss on her that still managed to curl her toes, despite her exhaustion. "I'll get him," he murmured.

"You're my hero."

He gave her another swift kiss. "And don't you forget it."

Two years after that night in the graveyard and she loved him more today than she thought possible. They'd dated a few months before he proposed, insisting that a lifetime of friendship and six years of foreplay was enough. She had gotten pregnant not long after the wedding.

His parents had been right. Nasty spirits showed up now and then, but Josie held them off with ease. Meanwhile, she resumed her chats with nicer spirits. Sometimes she was an ear for them, and sometimes they were for her. These days her biggest problem was sleep.

The phone rang. She jumped as the loud noise intruded into the silence of the early morning.

With a grumble, Josie snatched her cell from the nightstand. The caller ID told her nothing. "Hello?"

"Josie Evans?"

"Yes."

"My name is Delilah. I am the owner and operator for a firm called Brimstone, Inc."

"I'm not looking for work right now, thanks."

Before she could hang up, though, Delilah's next words stopped her. "I specialize in paranormal work. I hear you have a gift with ghosts."

Josie sucked in a breath. Was this lady for real? "I don't know what you're talking about."

"You do. But I also know that you still need some answers. Like how you make sure to keep the malevolent spirits out, if you can speak to other spirits like your brother's who aren't dead yet, and what else your abilities will allow you to do."

Whoa. She really did know. "Who told you about me?"

"Joyce Evans."

Josie narrowed her eyes. "She's dead." Who was this person?

"I know," said Delilah with a sigh. "Your mother-in-law can be quite persuasive though. Also I have a problem I think you can help solve. Are you interested?"

"Josie…" The whispered words yanked her attention to the corner of her room. She dropped the phone in her lap as Joyce waved a greeting.

She looked at her, then to the phone, then back at her. Slowly, Josie put the phone back up to her ear. "I'm listening."

THE END

Thank you so much for reading Josie and Bryce's story! I hope you enjoyed it. Would you like to read Rowan and Greyson's story, too? Then be sure to…

Read the next book
of the Brimstone Inc. Series:
BAIT N' WITCH

BAIT N' WITCH

BRIMSTONE INC. BOOK 4

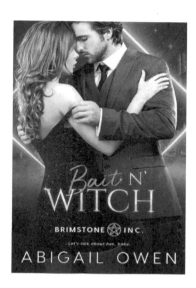

Let's talk about hex, baby!

Rowan McAuliffe has been hiding most of her life. Secretly trained in her powers by an unusual source, she'd been taught not to trust anyone. Especially other witches. However, after she was forced to perform a hateful act against her will, she now hides from the Covens Syndicate and their judgement.

Greyson Masters is the Syndicate's best hunter. On top of the danger of his job, Greyson is trying to raise his triplet daughters alone, budding new witches who display an alarming combined power no one understands. Too bad he doesn't have a clue how to deal with them.

Until Rowan walks in and the chaos settles for the first time in… well, ever.

Little does Greyson realize that his new nanny is the very witch he is hunting, and she's been hiding right under his nose this whole time.

READ BAIT N' WITCH NOW!

ALSO BY ABIGAIL OWEN

Don't miss the rest of Abigail's books...

PARANORMAL ROMANCE

INFERNO RISING

completed series

THE ROGUE KING

THE BLOOD KING

THE WARRIOR KING

THE CURSED KING

FIRE'S EDGE

completed series

THE MATE (free novella)

THE BOSS

THE ROOKIE

THE ENFORCER

THE PROTECTOR

THE TRAITOR

BRIMSTONE INC.

completed series

THE DEMIGOD COMPLEX

SHIFT OUT OF LUCK

A GHOST OF A CHANCE

BAIT N' WITCH

TRY AS I SMITE

HIT BY THE CUPID STICK

SHADOWCAT NATION

completed series | vintage titles

HANNAH'S FATE

ANDROMEDA'S FALL

SARAI'S FORTUNE

TIERYN'S FURY

SENECA'S FAITH

SVATURA

completed series | vintage titles

BLUE VIOLET

WHITE HYACINTH

CRIMSON DAHLIA

BLACK ORCHID

STANDALONE STORY

THE WOLF I WANT FOR CHRISTMAS

UPPER YA FANTASY ROMANCE

DOMINIONS TRILOGY

THE LIAR'S CROWN

THE STOLEN THRONE

THE SHADOWS RULE ALL

∼

For a suggested reading order,
go to Abigail's website...

abigailowen.com

∼

Abigail also writes contemporary romance as...
Kadie Scott (steamy) | Kristen McKanagh (sweet)

ABOUT THE AUTHOR

Multi-award-winning author, Abigail Owen, writes adult paranormal romance & upper YA/new adult fantasy romance. She loves plots that move hot and fast, feisty heroines with sass, heroes with heart, a dash of snark, and oodles of HEAs! Other titles include wife, mother, Star Wars geek, ex-competitive skydiver, spreadsheet lover, eMBA, organizational guru, Texan, Aggie, and chocoholic.

Abigail attempted to find a practical career by earning a degree in English Rhetoric (Technical Writing) and an MBA. However, she swiftly discovered that writing without imagination is not nearly as fun as writing with it.

Abigail currently resides in Austin, Texas, with her own

swoon-worthy hero, their angelic teenagers, and two adorable fur babies.

Don't miss a new release and
get in on insider fun like bonus content,
early announcements, and all my giveaways...

Subscribe to my newsletter:
SUBSCRIBE

Follow me in all the places...

http://www.abigailowen.com

Abbie's Awesome Nerds
(Private Facebook Group)

ACKNOWLEDGMENTS

Dear Reader,

As always, I have a ton of thanks that I owe to a wide support network of fantastic folks.

To the readers, thanks for the support, and hugs, and interest, and being awesome. And especially for reading my books! Josie and Bryce were so fun with their interactions given that she sees ghosts and he didn't know until recently. I hope you loved this as much as I loved writing it.

Thank you to my beta readers. Especially thank you to all the Awesome Nerds who volunteered and gave me the best feedback. I hope you'll see how much that helped! As always, thank you Mom! Your comments, edits, and support make me a better writer. The best gift you could ever give an author!

A very special thank you, as always, to my amazing husband and kids who put up with me living in my own head for hours, days, and even weeks at a time. Your support means more than I can say.

xoxo,
Abigail